Helme Heine

The Marvelous Journey Through the Night

TRANSLATED BY RALPH MANHEIM

Farrar, Straus & Giroux
New York

Every night
you start on a marvelous journey.
Without luggage, without passport,
without money.

When it's time to go, you make the secret sign.
You put your hand over your mouth and yawn.

Then along comes Sleep with his moon-lantern
and makes your eyelids droop.
    You can fight him off, you can jump
over tables and chairs.
    You can say you're hungry and thirsty,
you can demand to be told three long stories.

But in the end your eyes close,
no matter how big or strong or old you are.

The animals are going, too,
tame ones and wild ones, big ones
and little ones.
    With loud yawns, they tug at their chains
or shake the bars of their cages,
until Sleep comes and sets them free.

The fishes rise up from their oceans,
rivers, and lakes; some even come from aquariums.
They all follow Sleep.

You walk through the black night
with your eyes shut.
    But if you cheat, if you open them or blink,
you have to start your journey all over again.
    Don't be afraid, you won't lose your way.
    Sleep is watching over you,
he will guide your steps.

Sleep leads you on.
When you forget who you are
and what your name is—
then he calls his sister, Dream.

She drives away the darkness
and leads you to the paradise of dreams,
the Land of Heart's Desire.

If you meet a pirate with a wooden leg
walking across the ocean,
and there's a blind man beside him,
who's showing him the way—
then you're in paradise.

If you see a hare
who's not afraid of the hunter—
then you're in paradise.

If the world looks like a painted picture—
then you're in paradise.

And if you fall off the top of a steeple
and don't break your neck—
then you're in paradise.

Sleep and Dream
stay with you and protect you
all through the night.

Until morning, when the alarm clock
drives you out of paradise.
That's when your journey
into the day begins.